D1611288

Other Books in the SpenserNation Series:

Spenser Goes to Portland
Spenser Goes to St. Louis

# Spenser's Savannah

by Spenser and Mom
Illustrated by Amie Jacobsen

To the SpenserNation team and all of my friends back in Savannah - especially the illustration department at SCAD. ~A.J.

SpenserNation

Published by Simple Fish Book Company, LLC, 5500 Abercorn Street, Suite 32, Savannah, Georgia USA 31405

Spenser's books are produced by SpenserNation, a CSM company.



---

Library of Congress Cataloging-in-Publication Data
Spenser.
Spenser's Savannah/ by Spenser and Mom; illustrated by Amie Jacobsen.
p. cm.

SUMMARY: A small dog and his mother explore the history and geography of Savannah, GA.
Audience: Ages 4-7
ISBN-13: 978-0-9817598-4-5
[1. Savannah (Ga.)—Description and travel. 2. Savannah (Ga.)—History. 3. Savannah (Ga.)—Juvenile fiction. 4. Dogs—Juvenile fiction. 5. Travel—Juvenile fiction.] I. Title. II. Brooks, Melanie. III. Jacobsen, Amie, ill.
2009906834

Printed in China

---

For more information or additional copies, please go to www.spensernation.com.

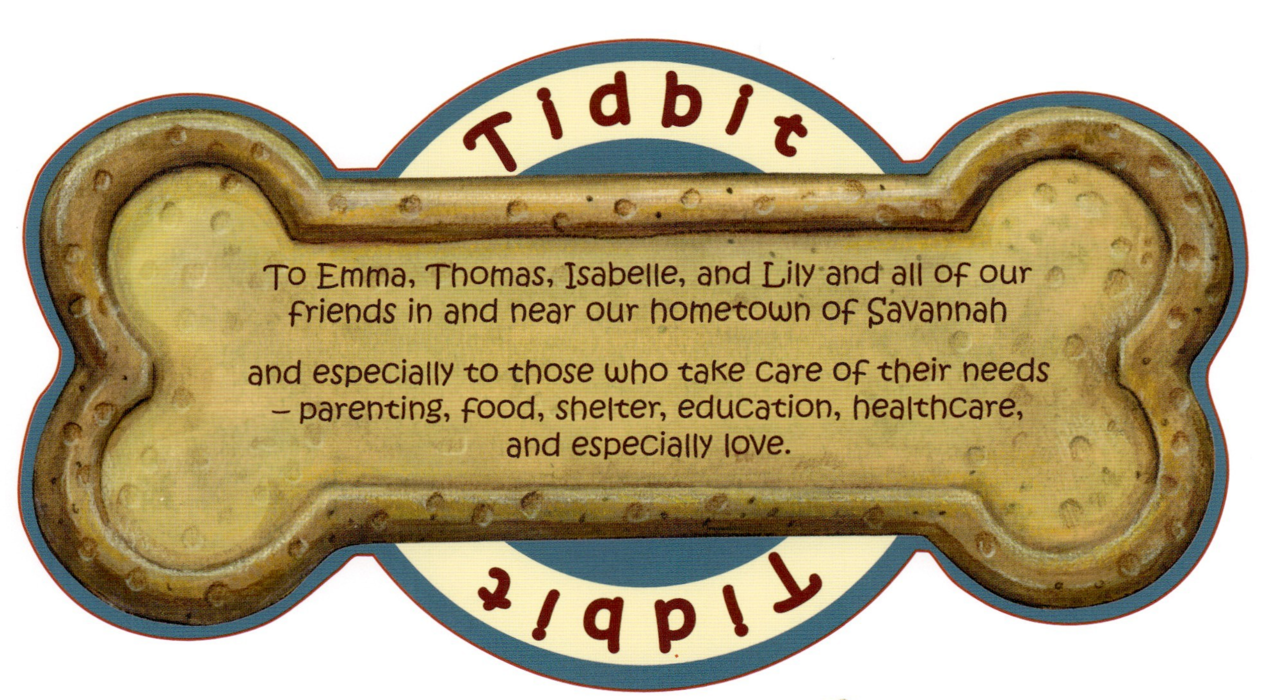


Spenser and Mom

"Spenser," Mom nudged me awake, "you need to get up and get moving if you want to go with me today. Grab your green beads and let's head for the car!"

I was awake – green beads! This was one of the great days of the year and what better place to celebrate than in my favorite city? It was St. Patrick's Day in Savannah, and Mom and I were going to watch the parade. I hopped out of bed, put on my beads and my favorite parade hat, and waited for Mom at the car.

Hello, in case we haven't met before, my name is Spenser. I am a dog, but don't tell my mom that because she thinks I am a real person. Mom is always ready to go exploring and because I am her best friend, she often takes me with her.

We write a story about each city we visit. Mom likes to be sure that I learn all I can about the history, geography, and culture of the area. This time we don't have to travel far to tell you about our hometown, Savannah, Georgia.

When Mom and I travel, we try to find a way to help children. In Savannah we have a special place where we go to help. Since it is all about kids, you will probably like learning about it.

Mom is also teaching me how to take care of our world, and so, in each story, we have a green lesson for me to learn and a new activity for me to do. I hope you will do these with me. It's always more fun to do things when you have friends who do them, too.

Mom and I have been to so many wonderful cities, and we want to tell you about all of them. But there is one special place that has a tight hold on our hearts, Savannah. Do you have one special city or town that makes you feel good all the way to your toes?

# Destination

Savannah is located in the state of Georgia, which is all the way to the right and way down near the bottom on a United States map. Savannah is on the Savannah River, right near the Atlantic Ocean. Do you see it?

One of my favorite things in Savannah is a huge globe. It is gigantic and has Savannah proudly marked on it.

"Georgia was the last of the original colonies to be founded, and Savannah is where the first people came," Mom explained as we made our way downtown. "Maybe we should take a few minutes before the fun starts and tell your friends about Savannah's special history."

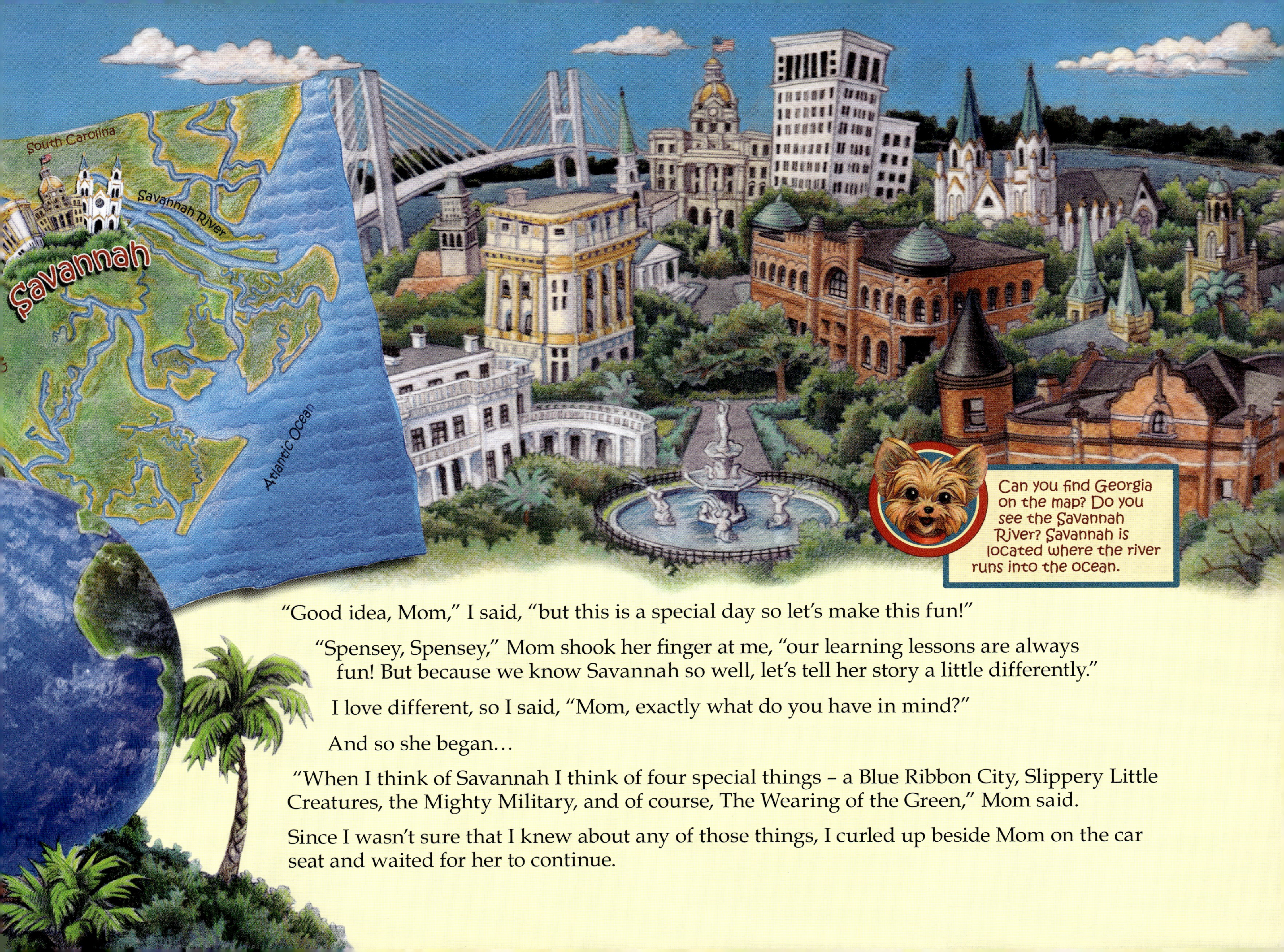


"Good idea, Mom," I said, "but this is a special day so let's make this fun!"

"Spensey, Spensey," Mom shook her finger at me, "our learning lessons are always fun! But because we know Savannah so well, let's tell her story a little differently."

I love different, so I said, "Mom, exactly what do you have in mind?"

And so she began…

"When I think of Savannah I think of four special things – a Blue Ribbon City, Slippery Little Creatures, the Mighty Military, and of course, The Wearing of the Green," Mom said.

Since I wasn't sure that I knew about any of those things, I curled up beside Mom on the car seat and waited for her to continue.

Blue Ribbon City
"Remember when you ran the race and got a blue ribbon, Spenser? Well, you got that ribbon because you were first. Ever since Savannah was founded almost 300 years ago, this city has been collecting first prize ribbons. That is why we call it a Blue Ribbon City."
"What kind of firsts are important, Mom?" I asked.
"Well," Mom replied, "besides being the first city in Georgia, Savannah was the first capital of Georgia. It was the first city drawn on a piece of paper before anyone even came to this part of the New World."
"Wow," I said, "that sounds pretty cool. What other blue ribbons does Savannah have, Mom?"
Mom continued, "The list goes on and on. There are things that made business in Savannah begin to grow, Spenser."
1 The first steamship to cross the Atlantic ocean was the Steamship Savannah.
1 The first cotton machine was made in Savannah.
Tidbit
The S.S. Savannah was the first steamship to cross the Atlantic Ocean. The N.S. Savannah was the first nuclear powered ship.
Tidbit
1 The first experimental or test garden was in Savannah. The planners wanted to know what would grow well in this part of the New World so they made plans to practice with different things.
Peach
Indigo
Olive
Rice
Cotton

"And let's give first prize ribbons to the people who came to Savannah from other countries wanting to start their own churches. Providing a place to worship was important to those early settlers of Savannah."

And Mom said, "Some blue ribbons just made life better for the people of Savannah."

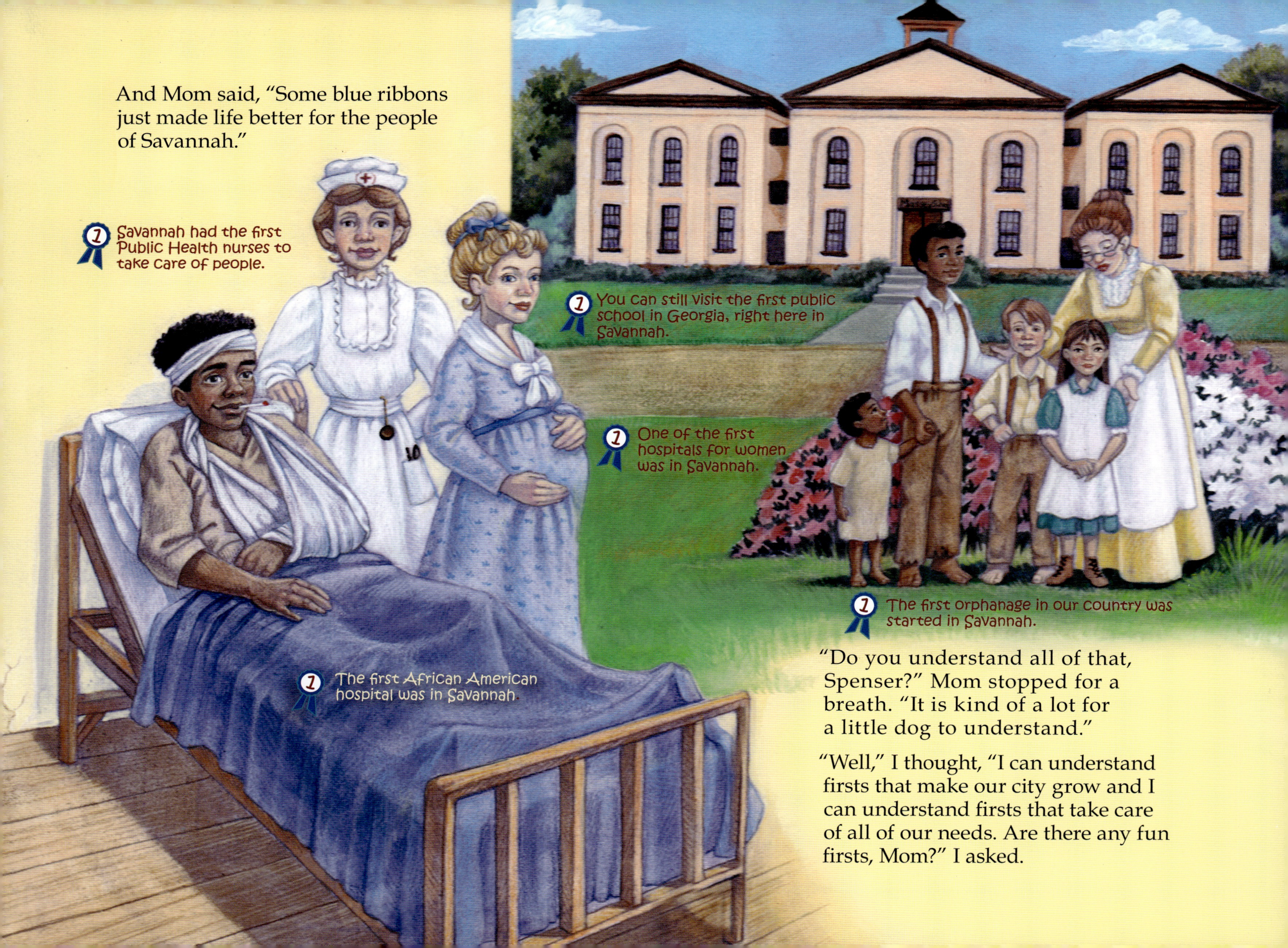


"Do you understand all of that, Spenser?" Mom stopped for a breath. "It is kind of a lot for a little dog to understand."

"Well," I thought, "I can understand firsts that make our city grow and I can understand firsts that take care of all of our needs. Are there any fun firsts, Mom?" I asked.

"Of course, you smart dog," Mom laughed. "Savannah has plenty of blue ribbons for fun things.
"And, all of these blue ribbons are pretty good reasons to be proud of Savannah, aren't they, Spensey?" Mom finished.
Can you think of special things about your hometown? Everyone's hometown is special in its own way. You should be proud of your hometown. List some firsts about your hometown or state or your school or church. Even in your family, you can probably find some firsts.
TELFAIR
ACADEMY OF ARTS AND SCIENCES
1
The south's first art museum and first garden for the blind were both in Savannah.
1
The first golf course in America was here.
1
And, if you drive down to the beach, you can see the first lighthouse on the southern coast.
1912
2010
1950
1
The first Girl Scout troop was started in Savannah.
Tidbit
Juliette Gordon Low started the first Girl Scout troop in Savannah after visiting England and meeting the man who started the Boy Scouts.
Tidbit
1
The first fire department with trucks was in Savannah.
How many Savannah firsts did Mom and Spenser talk about?

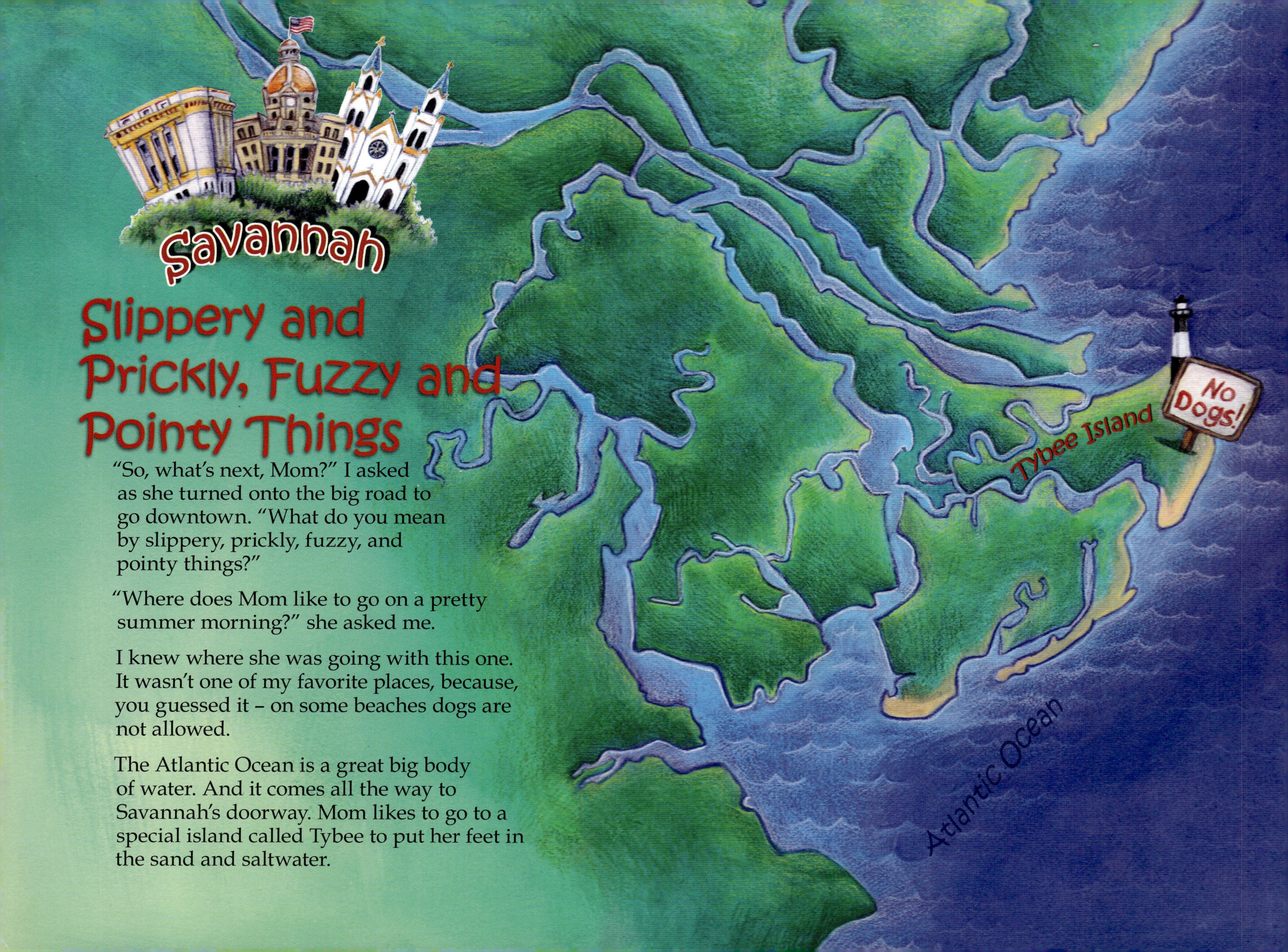


# Slippery and Prickly, Fuzzy and Pointy Things

"So, what's next, Mom?" I asked as she turned onto the big road to go downtown. "What do you mean by slippery, prickly, fuzzy, and pointy things?"

"Where does Mom like to go on a pretty summer morning?" she asked me.

I knew where she was going with this one. It wasn't one of my favorite places, because, you guessed it – on some beaches dogs are not allowed.

The Atlantic Ocean is a great big body of water. And it comes all the way to Savannah's doorway. Mom likes to go to a special island called Tybee to put her feet in the sand and saltwater.

Have you ever been to a beach? Sometimes Mom takes me to a special dog beach. The sand feels funny and the waves are pretty cool. They just keep coming and coming. Mom tells me they are created by the moon. I don't understand that right now, but she says I will when I get a little older.

Mom said, "Savannah also has many rivers that go into or come out of that big ocean. There are animals that live in rivers and animals that live in the ocean. Some of the animals are food for us, and some are food for fish or other water animals. Can you tell your friends about your favorites, Spensey?"

Well, as you would guess, my very favorites are the kinds you can eat – slippery shrimp, prickly crabs, and pointy oysters! And just about every kind of fish you can name (of course not goldfish, because they are pets like me).

But, I also like water animals that I can't eat. Sometimes when Mom visits the ocean, she brings back sand dollars that look like a big dollar coin and starfish that look like stars from the sky. I love those. Both of them are a little fuzzy on the bottom. The sad part is that by the time I see them, the animal part of them is already dead.

"Spenser," Mom said, "the Atlantic Ocean near Savannah also has dolphins. Sometimes we can see them from the beach. Sometimes we have to go out on a boat to see them."

Tidbit

Oceans and rivers provide lots of food for people all over the world. Seafood is especially good for children.

Tidbit

“What are dolphins, Mom?” I asked. I don’t think I have ever seen dolphins.

“They look like big fish, Spenser, but they are really mammals like us. They can be very, very big. Dolphins love to swim and dive and play in the ocean, so they are fun to watch. They have slippery skin, a pointy nose, prickly fins, and a fuzzy tongue.”

“So, Mom, they are everything we’re talking about rolled into one animal,” I said with a smile. I like it when I can figure things out, don’t you?

“That’s a good way to look at it, smart Spenser,” Mom laughed.

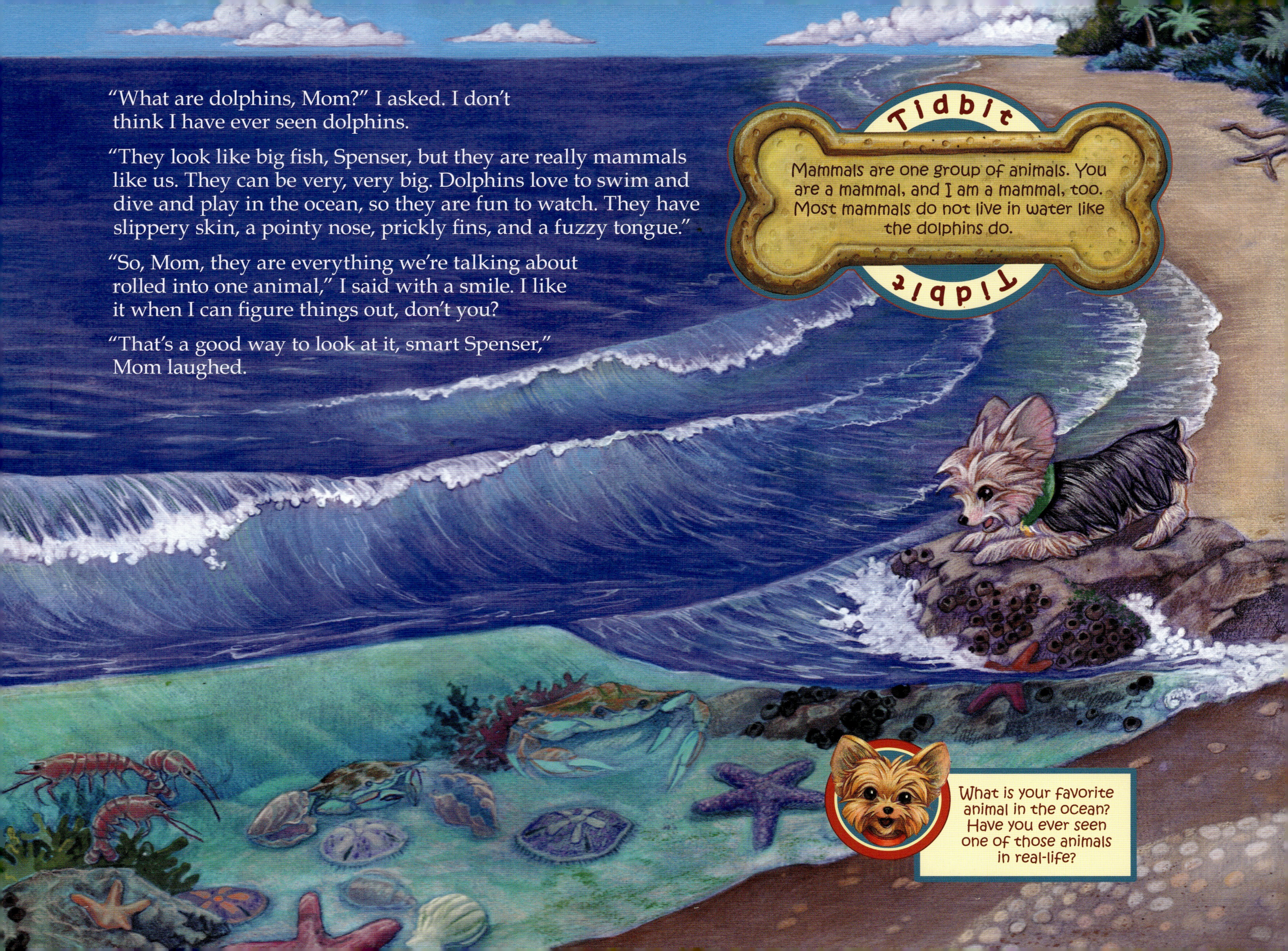

Mom was looking for a parking place as she finished the water animals story. Parking is always difficult during the St. Patrick's Day celebration. As she drove, she said, "Let's tell your friends about our Mighty Military. You know we will see lots of military men and women in the parade today."

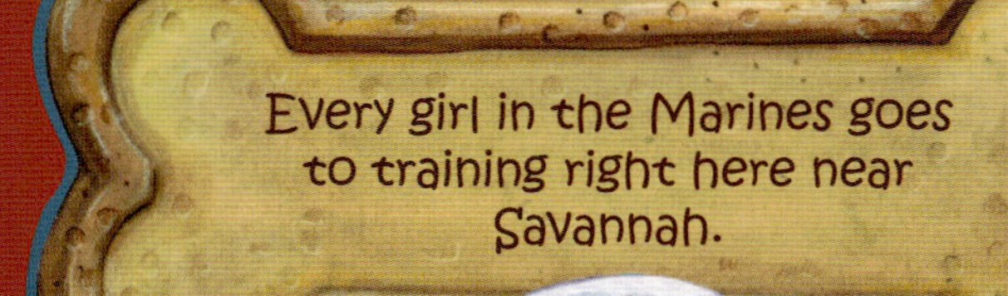


Tidbit

The 3rd Infantry Division of the Army at Ft. Stewart, near Savannah, has one of the most successful war records of any division of the Army.

Tidbit

The 8th Air Force was formed in Savannah and went overseas right away to help beat the Germans in World War II.

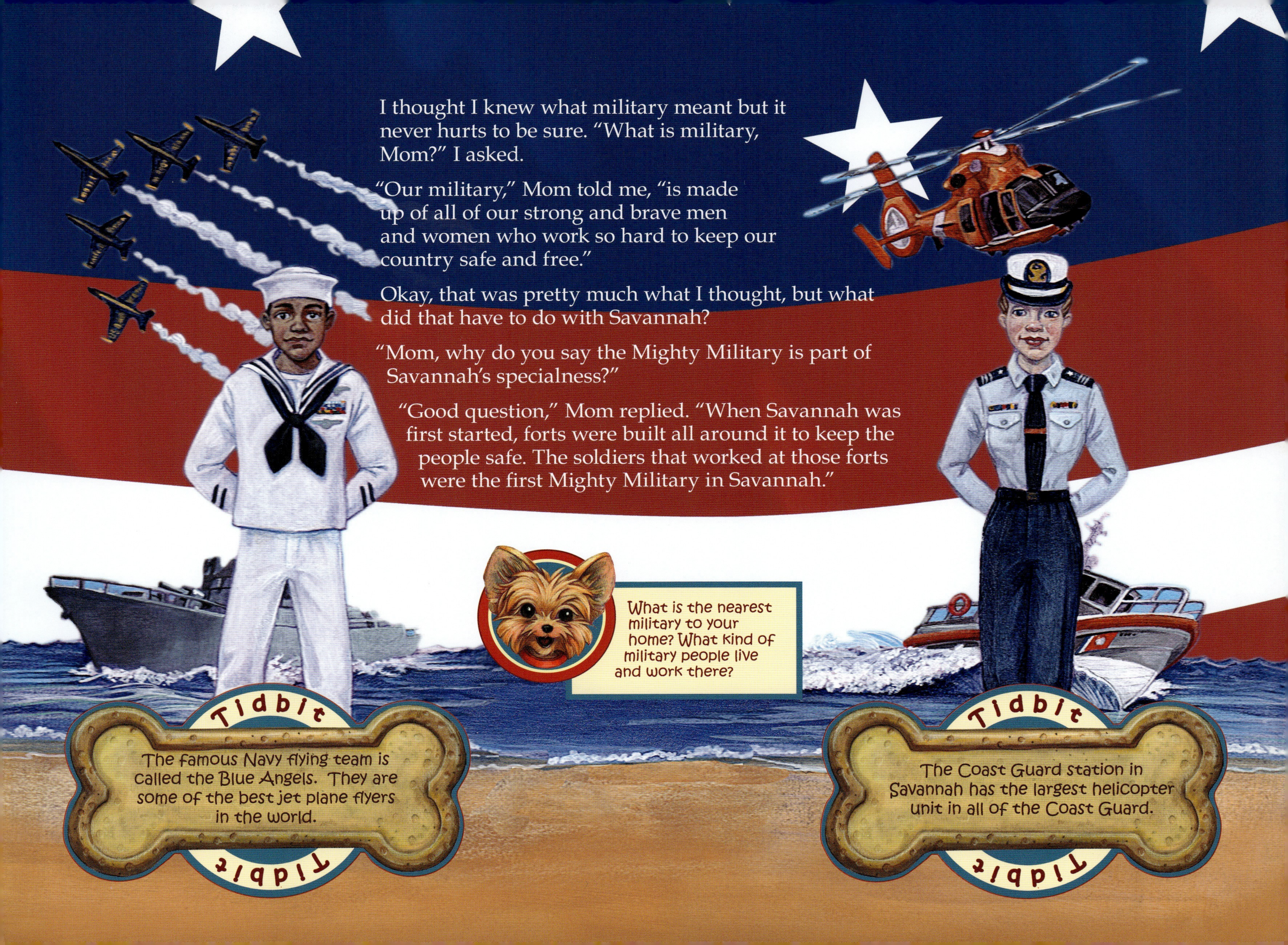

I thought I knew what military meant but it never hurts to be sure. "What is military, Mom?" I asked.

"Our military," Mom told me, "is made up of all of our strong and brave men and women who work so hard to keep our country safe and free."

Okay, that was pretty much what I thought, but what did that have to do with Savannah?

"Mom, why do you say the Mighty Military is part of Savannah's specialness?"

"Good question," Mom replied. "When Savannah was first started, forts were built all around it to keep the people safe. The soldiers that worked at those forts were the first Mighty Military in Savannah."

What is the nearest military to your home? What kind of military people live and work there?

**Tidbit**

The famous Navy flying team is called the Blue Angels. They are some of the best jet plane flyers in the world.

**Tidbit**

The Coast Guard station in Savannah has the largest helicopter unit in all of the Coast Guard.

"Now," Mom continued, "Savannah is one of the few cities in the whole country that has every kind of military right here!"

"Every kind?" I asked.

"Yes," she said, "we have every kind."

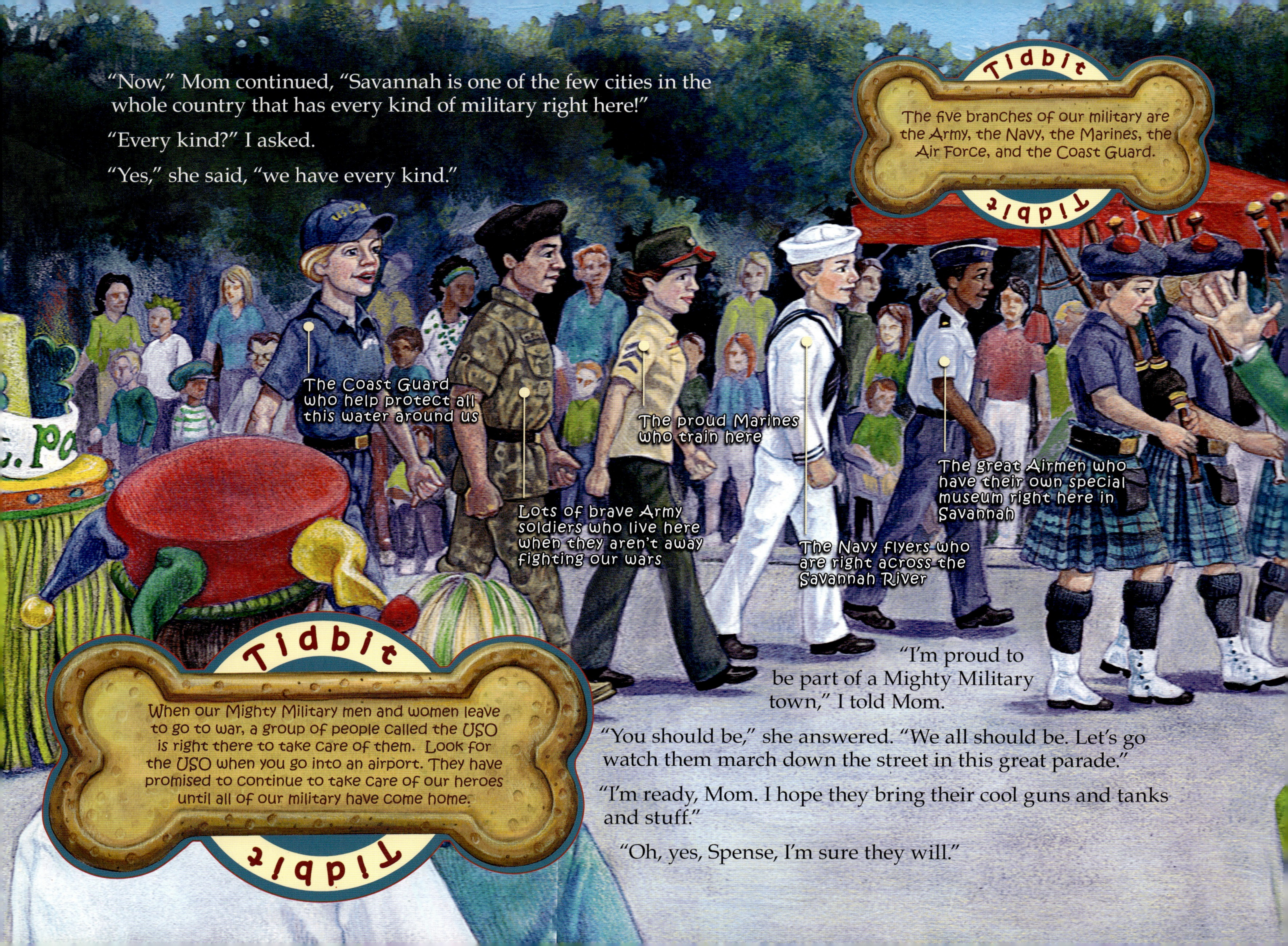


"I'm proud to be part of a Mighty Military town," I told Mom.

"You should be," she answered. "We all should be. Let's go watch them march down the street in this great parade."

"I'm ready, Mom. I hope they bring their cool guns and tanks and stuff."

"Oh, yes, Spense, I'm sure they will."

# The Wearing Of The Green

And finally! The parade! All around me people were wearing green – hats, shirts, and beads. Some of them had even colored their hair green. Everyone was very excited.

"Why is St. Patrick's Day so important to Savannah, Mom?" I asked.

"St. Patrick is special to the people of Ireland, and the people of Ireland are special to Savannah. They came to Savannah in the early days of our city. They were hard-working people who had come to find a new home. Their hometowns in Ireland were struggling with a potato famine."

"What is a potato famine, Mom?"

"A famine is when there is not enough food and people are starving. The Irish people ate a lot of potatoes, so when there were no potatoes to eat many people died. The potato famine lasted six years. A lot of the Irish people came to our country to find food to eat.

"The Irish people were happy in Savannah, Spenser. And Savannah was happy to have these family-loving, church-going, fun-sharing people in our city."

"And on St. Patrick's Day, we are all Irish," I said, "right, Mom?" Come on with us as we get to share their very special day.

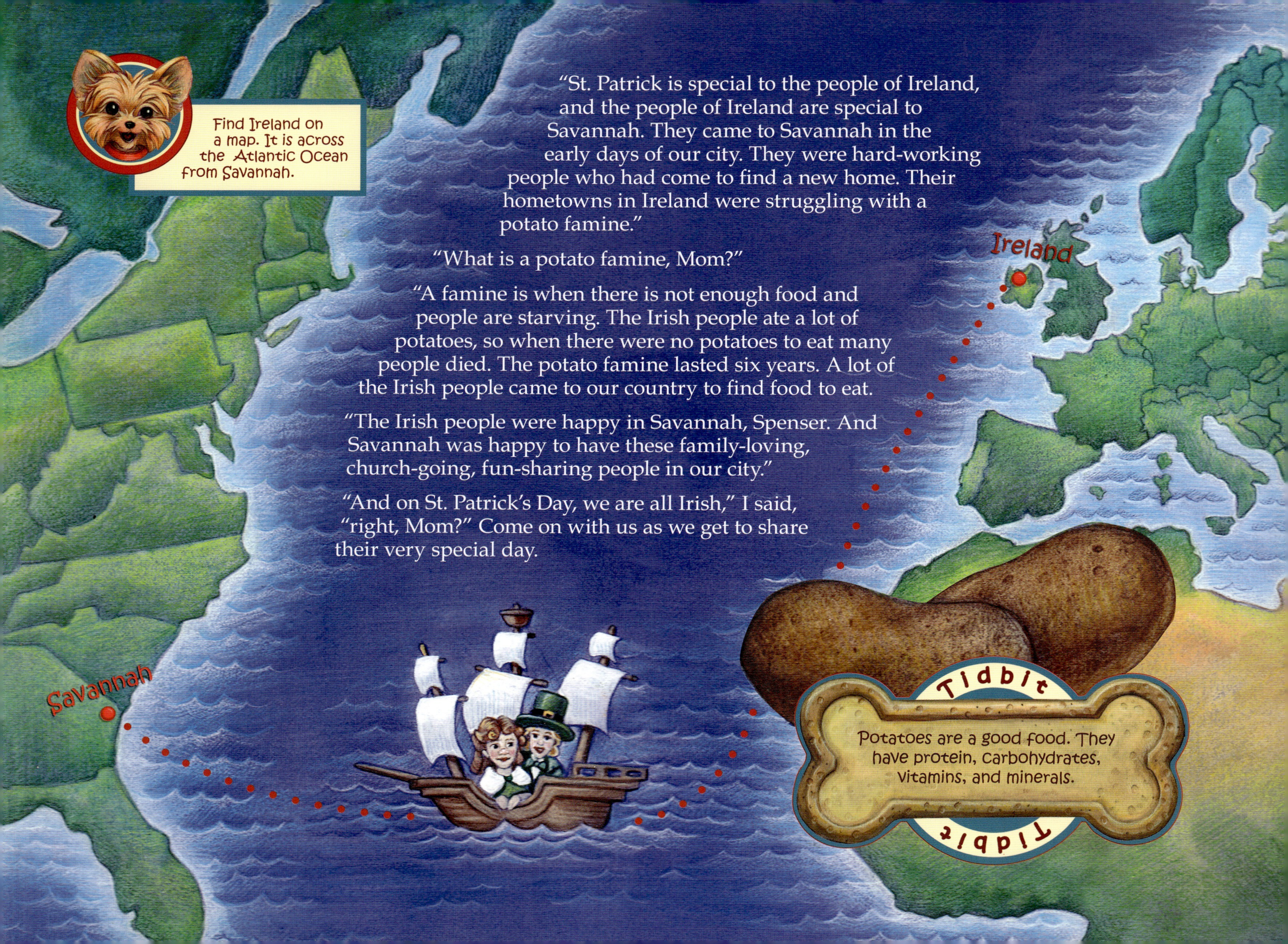

I love the parade. Policemen lead the way with their blue lights flashing. Marching bands, pretty girls, soldiers and sailors, firemen, horses dressed up fancy, and lots of Irish families come down the street. It is very important for Irish families to walk together in the parade. Baby carriages, wagons, and strollers carry the little Irish people. Everyone is part of this celebration. If you ever visit Savannah on St. Patrick's Day, you can be Irish, too.

Mom and I always have a great time. The parade is very long and sometimes I get tired, but I never want to leave early. I get sad when it is over. Do you get sad when fun things have to end?

"Erin Go Bragh," Mom said, "means 'Ireland Forever.' It is what we say on St. Patrick's Day."

So, Erin Go Bragh, my friends, it's been fun being Irish with you today!

Shamrocks are also special on St. Patrick's Day. It is a three-leafed clover and a symbol of Ireland. See if you can find one or a picture of one.

# Kids Café

"Mom, is today a Kids Café day?" I asked as we walked back towards the car. "The parade was fun, but I think it is time for us to help some hungry children."

"Not too tired, Spenser?" Mom asked.

"Never, Mom, I'm ready."

Mom and I are working hard to make sure hungry children get good meals. In Savannah our special project is Kids Café. Kids Cafés are great places where kids can go after school, get a snack, get help with their homework, play games or do arts and crafts, and then get a really good hot meal for dinner.

The first Kids Café was in Savannah, but now there are programs all across the country. It is the largest kids feeding program in the United States. We love it because it takes care of so many hungry children.

Mom and I have our own job with the children. We help them learn about eating good food, but you know me, I want to have fun while we are learning. So we play games and laugh and learn. The learning part keeps Mom happy.

Today our trip is right across town to the Kayton Homes Kids Café where almost 100 children come each day for fun and dinner.

Mom and I played Hunger Bingo with the children, a game that Mom likes because it talks about good food. You can download it from my website and play it, too.

Dinner looked good, too. Beef stew and rice, corn, applesauce, and milk. We talked about how important milk is for children's health.

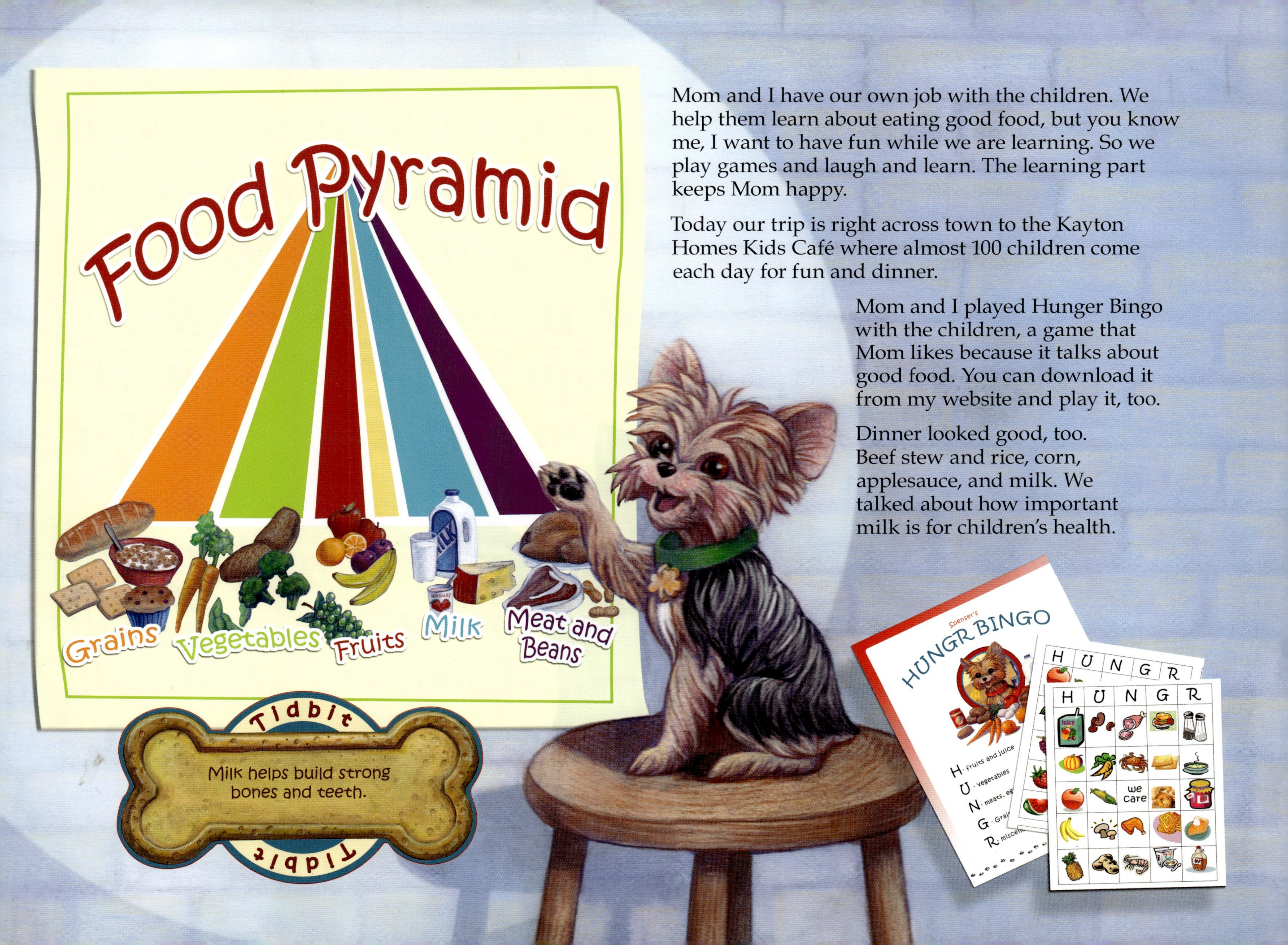

# Taking Care of Our World

Have you seen those cool bags in grocery stores? The kind you don't throw away or recycle but use each time you go grocery shopping?

Mom says those are very good for our environment. The problem is she can't remember to take them to the grocery store, so we have decided that is going to be my job.

I am going to remember to put them back in the car after we empty them each time. Then they will always be there when we need them. Could you help your mom or dad and do that, too?

You can even visit the store on my website and buy special SpenserNation grocery bags to use when you shop.

Do you have reusable grocery bags at your house? Talk to your parents about a plan for you to be in charge of the bags. It's fun being in charge of something.

**Tidbit**

Plastic and paper grocery bags use up our resources and fill up our landfills. Reusable bags are much better for our earth.

Hope you enjoyed learning about my hometown. Let me know if you ever come this way to visit. Savannah loves visitors and so do I.

Until next time, be good, my friends at SpenserNation,

Spenser and Mom

# My hometown foodbank, America's Second Harvest of Coastal Georgia

America's Second Harvest of Coastal Georgia uses food donations to feed hungry people and to help communities. Food comes from businesses, organizations, and schools but especially from the people of the Savannah area as they participate in food drives and donation programs. Major corporations also make donations to ASHCG. This year we received 67,600 pounds of food from Smithfield Foods' "Helping Hungry Homes" initiative and 8,000 pounds of tuna and salmon from the StarKist Tuna contest.

Hunger gnaws at individual bellies, but it consumes communities. When individuals suffer, communities suffer.

America's Second Harvest of Coastal Georgia serves 21 coastal Georgia counties providing food to children, families, seniors, the homeless, and those at risk for hunger. Through our Kids Café program, Lunch Box program, Brown Bag for the Elderly, Mobile Food Pantry, and our Community Kitchen, we provide assistance and long-term solutions to hunger and poverty.

## Facts About Hunger:

More than 66% of children in coastal Georgia are at risk for hunger.

Kids Cafés started in Savannah, Georgia and now serve more than 110,000 children an evening meal in 45 states throughout our nation. In coastal Georgia, there are 34 Kids Cafés serving more than 2,500 area children.

The Lunch Box Program, also a Savannah initiative, provides meals to children in rural areas that do not have access to much needed food.

The Brown Bag Program for the Elderly provides a bag of groceries, including some protein items, delivered to our most needy senior citizens during the last week of the month. This is the time when many Social Security checks have run out and these people are at risk for hunger.